MW01673204

EXCORIATE

PIAMO

ISBN 979-8950178009 (paperback edition)
First printing 2026

Story and cover design by piamo
Cover art from *Swamp Scene* by Joseph Rusling Meeker
Proofreading by Mel C.
Interior illustrations by catallarii
Formatting by subvertebra

They is, they is, they is.

— *Tobias Wolff, Bullet in the Brain*

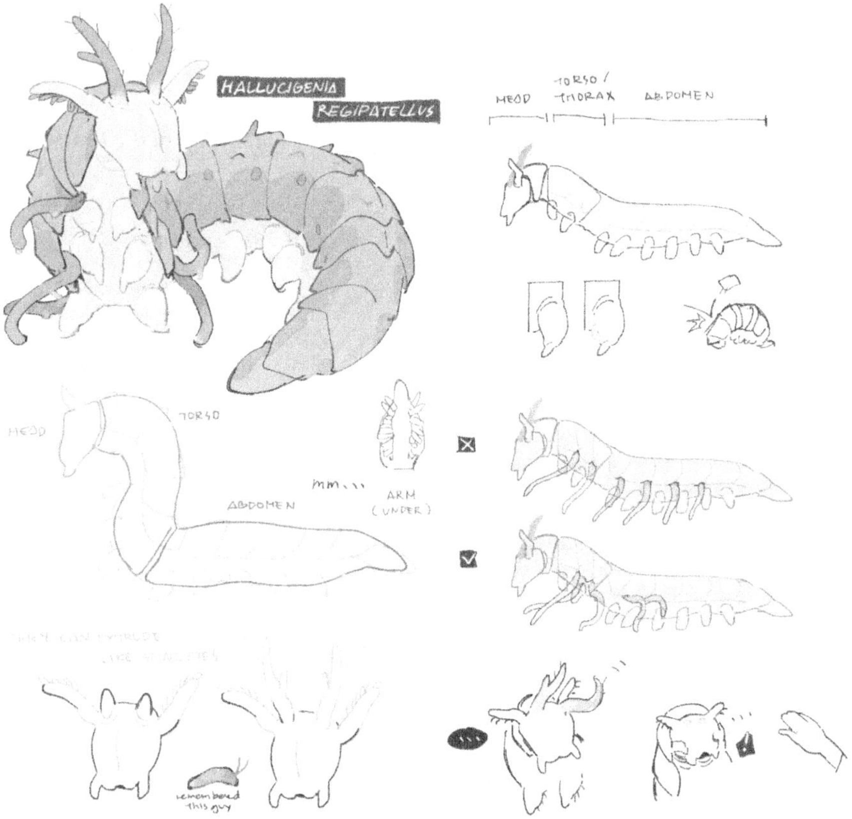
HALLUCIGENIA
REGIPATELLUS
HEAD
TORSO / THORAX
ABDOMEN
HEAD
TORSO
ABDOMEN
mm...
ARM (UNDER)
remembered this guy

AMercyofCrows [21:13]: (📎 File Attachment)

cluecat [21:15]: What is this? You didn't get hacked did you…

AMercyofCrows [21:15]: just open it

cluecat [21:16]: Windows is telling me it's a virus. >_>

AMercyofCrows [21:16]: it's not a virus.

cluecat [21:17]: OK. I guess I click download anyway? One sec.

AMercyofCrows [21:21]: hello?

cluecat [21:37]: Hal, this is really sweet. I can tell you put a lot of time into this. But I'm already going to Winter Formal with Oliver. Sorry, I thought I told you ;;

AMercyofCrows [21:38]: ah, got it. no problem

cluecat [21:38]: It really means a lot to me that you asked! You're a great friend. <3

Hal pushed his laptop aside. The good news was, it had only taken him ten minutes to make that executable in C++. All it did was open the command prompt and spit out a poem with some ASCII art for decoration. He'd figured she'd reject him like this, so he'd made sure not to put too much effort into it. Siobhan and him had been friends since middle school. Just because she held his hand at the graduation dance didn't mean anything. Obviously.

Signal pinged with a few more messages. They were discussing AP English in the group chat. Hal ignored it. *Friendzoned.* At least he knew for sure now. And he wouldn't have to go through the hassle of finding some ugly tux to wear.

Something flaked off under his nail. He looked down at his fingertips.

Blood. Again.

He always kept a Kleenex box next to his second monitor. He tugged out a wad of tissues, cleaned his fingers off, and found the spot that was bleeding—a sore on his left cheek. It took a minute of holding the tissue against his skin before the bleeding stopped.

"There's fish sticks in the freezer if you want to heat some up in the microwave," his mom called the second he passed by the entry shower. She was hosing off his waders.

He backtracked. Scratch that, she was *throwing his waders in the trash.*

"Mom, don't."

"These things have been leaking for weeks." Her gloved finger tapped the heel, a spot where he'd duct taped a hole. The duct tape was in perfectly good condition, so he didn't know what her point was. "What about the new pair I got you?"

"I told you. They gave me blisters."

"Okay, well, these ones will give you literal multimodal hallucinations. Leave the new ones by the door, I'll return them next time I'm outside—and *Hal.*"

Frustrated, Hal backtracked again. He leered at the spot where his waders could be seen poking out of the trash. "What."

His mother motioned to her face and mouthed something. A reminder. *Use the finger mittens.*

⊙

They were out of Flamin' Hot Cheetos. Hal had entered the kitchen with zero intention of eating fish sticks for the nth day in a row, and now he had no choice. The microwave spun, rattling glass. He scrolled Reddit.

u/eroplane99 (5 minutes ago)

NATURE IS HEALING (NOT!!!!) [memes] [graphic imagery]

u/zooom_zooom (17 minutes ago)

ELI5: How did the glaciers melt so fast? It feels like everything was fine one day, and now all of a sudden I'm living in a swamp?? I thought carbon capture was supposed to fix this shit. [science]

u/awawa125 (2 hours ago)

why the FUCK do people queue up if they're just gonna go AFK? been playing Valorant for 2 months and i already feel like quitting [discussion]

u/holdtheapplecause (1 day ago)

Is it safe to go to Springfield alone if you don't have desiccant? I've been affected by the shortage too, but my sister lives there and needs supplies. Are their xenopillars really worse than Portland's? [question]

Beeep. Beeep. Beeep.

There were still no clean bowls. The kitchen sink had been backing up all week. The guy who lived a street over had said it was happening at his place, too. Probably nymphs gumming up the city's plumbing. Again. Hal grabbed a paper towel square and made a nest in his hoodie pocket to dump his fish sticks into. They skated off the microwave's glass plate way too smoothly for his liking. He prodded them. Still frozen.

"Microwave's busted," Hal said.

"Again?"

His mom shook out her graying hair, then started fumbling with the microwave's guts. She smelled bad. Really bad. That's what being decked out in waders and slash-proof gear did to you. Hal didn't think he smelled much better, but the only thing he'd done was rot in front of a computer all day "attending" class.

"Pretty sure I can fix this."

"You can't fix it, Mom."

"I fixed it last time, didn't I?" She unplugged the microwave, then plugged it back in.

"Reddit says there's capacitors inside that can arc and kill you even if it's detached from a power source. And the magnetron has a beryllium oxide insulator, which is toxic to inhale. Don't try."

A defeated sigh. "Fine. We'll heat them up on the stove. Just give me a second to grab the propane."

"It's fine. I'm going back to my room."

"Are you sure?" The concern in her voice followed him down the hallway. He couldn't escape fast enough. "Hon, is there something upsetting you? I noticed you're picking more than usual—"

With a *BANG*, the door slammed shut behind him.

His room was pretty much a coat closet. It was filled with junk like a coat closet, it smelled funky like a coat closet, and, like a coat closet, there was barely enough space for a mattress inside. Hal gnawed a barely defrosted fish stick and plugged in his gaming mouse. The usual rainbow LEDs didn't light up. He unplugged it, then plugged it back in. Nothing.

Bangznut [21:55]: u tried new batteries?

AMercyofCrows [21:57]: it's a wired mouse...

Bangznut [21:57]: mybe reinstall drivers

Bangznut [21:57]: u could see if ur mom can fix it

AMercyofCrows [22:04]: nevermind. I found the issue.

AMercyofCrows [22:05]: (📎Image Attachment)

Bangznut [22:05]: are those TEETH marks?

Bangznut [22:06]: looks like ratatouille helped himself to ur spicy grass

Bangznut [22:06]: LOL

Bangznut [22:06]: i'm kidding dude. prob just the usual wear n tear

Bangznut [22:07]: think u can play val with the trackpad?

Hal pushed his laptop aside. He'd successfully stripped all the breading off the frozen fish stick in his mouth, but the fish part was rock solid. He massaged his forehead, his cheeks, his chin.

By end of June, he would be graduated. High school was supposed to suck. That's what everyone always said. Was it supposed to make him feel better? In a weird way, middle school had been worse. At least over these last four years, he hadn't had to physically show up to class.

Seeing his peers in person would probably suck, too. Winter Formal could go to hell.

When Signal pinged again, Hal peeled his forehead off his desk. One new message from Siobhan. He knew he would feel like shit if he checked it, and he checked it anyway because he was an idiot. Obviously.

cluecat [22:16]: You doing OK, Hal?

"I'm fine," he said aloud.

And even if that weren't true, the only thing he needed to *be* fine was a bag of fucking Flamin' Hot Cheetos. And a new USB cable. Both of which were basically within walking distance. And like hell he was going to give himself blisters running the smallest fucking errand when he was old enough to fucking FUCK—not that that was going to happen in this lifetime, not when he couldn't even get his own best friend to accompany him to a dance that didn't have to and never was supposed to mean anything.

AMercyofCrows [22:20]: give me ~20-30 min

Bangznut [22:21]: ur mom got ur mouse working?!>

AMercyofCrows [22:21]: yes

Bangznut [22:21]: helllll yea

Bangznut [22:22]: (>'-')> <('-'<) ^( )^ (>'-')> <('-'<)

AMercyofCrows [22:24]: I just need to grab food. Brb

⊙

The purr of the Jon boat was quiet enough that the sleeping ducks kept on sleeping. Enshittification was everywhere, but at least it hadn't messed up trolling motors too badly. Hal watched the house recede behind him. He puttered out of the neighborhood. It was late enough and cold enough that barely anyone was out. Springfield was a sleepy little town, especially with people getting picked off every other day. But where weren't people getting picked off? He wasn't worried; he had a rifle loaded with desiccant. His mom was basically a hoarder, but it worked out that the stuff she hoarded was usually guns, toilet paper, and ammo.

According to Google, the 7-Eleven off Main Street was open until 11 p.m. He couldn't remember if this location took points or just cash. He only had his phone on him.

It turned out that didn't even matter, because the closer he got, he realized that the shop's windows had all been busted in. A bow rider was peeling away, an ATM loaded in the back. Looters.

It wasn't like Hal hadn't done his own fair share of looting. When everyone else was doing it, there wasn't much of a reason to hold back. Generally, unless you were going for the pharmacies, it was more trouble than it was worth getting the iron bars off the windows. But these assholes had politely done the work for him.

Hal killed the motor. He readied his rifle and did the usual pebble check.

One foot. *Plip.*

Five feet. *Plip.*

Twenty-something feet. *Plip.*

When nothing spat a faceful of slime at him, he hopped out, tied the Jon boat to a rusty bike rack sticking out of the muck, and started wading towards the 7-Eleven's doors.

The streetlights were out. They had been out for the past eight years, ever since the town flooded like a run-down water park—the kind kids drowned in the wave pools of. The looming posts were just an annoying reminder that people used to have sidewalks to walk on. Technically, there still were sidewalks if you went far enough east. But what was the point? You'd be lugging around a metric ton of water instead. Xenopillar slime fell apart in water. They could swim, but being in water was the safest place you could be.

Being out at night was sort of a bad idea all around, though. Because as blind as xenopillars were, humans didn't have great night vision either.

In and out, Hal thought. He could make out the chip aisle from here. There were Pringles at least.

He splashed towards the stairs, then clambered onto dry land. It should come as no surprise that it was too dark for him to see the square of silver that had floated up to the water's surface in his wake: a piece of duct tape mingling with all the other garbage.

⊙

Tiktok had a blast with them when they first started showing up in Alaska. *Hallucigenia Regipatellus,* a distant ancestor of the velvet worm. They came out of the melting glaciers, just like Vice always said they would, squishy rainbow millipede-looking critters just a few centimeters long. Who could have guessed the hormones in our water would do something the Cambrian Period couldn't. Once they got to be the size of German Shepherds, people switched from calling them "werms" to "lobopods." And the first time a kid got eaten by one, the name "xenopillars" took off, even though the prefix "xeno-" was, according to everyone's AP English teacher this side of the Mississippi, misapplied. The worms were here first.

It was up to each state to figure out what to do with their Hallucigenids. Even Oregon had tried the bioengineered parasite method. And look how that had turned out.

Since then, four years had passed, and the term "werms" had come back into circulation. It was a coping thing. They were the size of horses, and they reproduced fast. You could kill them with a desiccant bullet between the eyes, but they could kill you right back by melting you with digestive acid.

Hal was an excellent shot though. His friends always joked he would make a good school shooter. So he wasn't overly concerned.

Slimy glass crunched underfoot. The 7-Eleven's iron bars were on the floor, having been sawed off. The door was gone. Hal tossed a few more pebbles, then stepped inside.

He found a pack of cheapo USB cables by the cash register. Or, at least, the spot where a cash register should have been. Only three bags of party-sized Flamin' Hot Cheetos would fit into his backpack. He stuffed a capsule of M&M Minis into his waders' chest pocket. The looters from earlier had cut the power, so he had to fumble around with a flashlight, which only made it harder to see given that he had fingerprints all over his goggles. The remaining question was where the underpaid retail guy was when all this went down—

"H-hey! Over here!"

Hal spun around. The beam of his flashlight ricocheted off the refrigerators lining the back wall, leaving him momentarily blinded.

Technically, you didn't need to see to swing a loaded gun around, but it definitely wasn't good practice. Hal knew his sophomore year survival ed teacher would be screaming at him for this. He blinked away the purple glare in his vision. Yeah, definitely screaming. Lying on the floor, trapped in a puddle of clear sludge, was a guy wearing one of those 7-Eleven polos, staring down the barrel of Hal's rifle with wide eyes.

"Christ," Hal breathed, deflating.

The slime on the guy's body had already hardened; it looked like Elmer's glue, which meant the consistency was like vulcanized rubber, which meant it had been ejected over three minutes ago. That the guy wasn't covered in digestive acid too was mind-boggling.

"You're pretty lucky," Hal said. He unclipped a canister from his belt and tossed it to 7-Eleven Guy, who at least had one hand not glued to the floor. The guy caught it, but kept gaping at Hal like a fish.

"What," Hal said.

7-Eleven Guy's irises were red. He had shaggy white hair that reached his shoulders. Albinism? Whatever. Swiveling his gun left and right, Hal watched out of the corner of his eye while the guy sprayed himself down with the canister, jerking his limbs as the slime started to soften. He was skinny, like a badly drawn stick figure. Definitely Hal's age. Probably younger.

"I just didn't think I was going to get my ass saved by a kid," 7-Eleven Guy said, finally breaking the silence. "Speaking of which, you should maybe hit the road. It might still—"

Hal scoffed. "If there was a werm in here, you'd be dead. Those looters scared it off." He pointed with his toe, adding, "Start from the waist and work down."

"Hah, right. I remember learning survival stuff in high school. I guess the universe thought I needed a refresher... Er, what's your name?"

"Hal. Yours?"

"Thom." The moment the guy said it, Hal caught the name tag pinned to the front of his shirt. The light reflecting off it hurt his eyes. "Do you go to school around here?" Thom asked. His right leg made a loud sucking sound as he worked to dislodge it from the melting goo.

Hal turned his flashlight down. Jesus, the beam on this thing was like a laser. "I graduated a few years ago," he said.

It wasn't like him to lie. Imagine if he *had* graduated a few years ago, though. Still stuck in Springfield, still living with his mom. No way. He needed to join the Peace Corps.

"We're probably the same age, then." More sucking sounds. Thom's left leg was coming free. "What do you miss the most?"

It was a good question. The answer, surprisingly, had nothing to do with kissing Siobhan. What Hal actually had missed out on was sneaking past the local swimming pool to finally locate that one secret fort someone had built and abandoned. The one with the whiteboard in it. He wished he had caught more rolly pollies and bartered for more Otter Pops. He couldn't blame the xenopillars. It was just that he wasn't a kid anymore, so that was the end of that.

"Uh." Hal blinked. His breath was fogging up his goggles. "What do I miss the most *about what.*"

"I dunno. Everything. I've been stuck in here a while. Like, longer than you might guess. I've had a lot of time to think. So I was wondering what kind of stuff you wish you'd done, things you wish you'd said, that sort of thing." Thom plopped his butt down on the slick linoleum floor. He mussed his hair, then ran a hand across his face. "Yeesh. My back hurts."

Hal stepped closer. Was this guy high or something? High. High school. Ha-ha. "Don't touch your face," he said. "You have slime on your hands. It's a—"

"I know. It's a hallucinogenic." Thom lifted his hand. It was hard to tell exactly how Hal knew he was lifting his hand, given that he'd turned his flashlight off completely. He watched Thom lick his palm. His tongue was pink.

"What does it taste like?" Hal blurted.

Thom laughed. His red eyes glistened as he extended his hand. "Would you like to find out?"

It didn't occur to Hal that it made no sense the way Thom was dressed. No mask, no goggles, no gloves, no waders, no gear, no gun. Just a polo, jeans, and sneakers. When was the last time he had seen a stranger's face IRL? You didn't leave your house not wearing PPE. Not unless you were a figment of some person's imagination and didn't actually exist. But, at the time, Hal hadn't noticed the slime pooling at his ankles either, or the sound of a nearby invertebrate undulating. The rifle had already slipped out of his hands. He must have looked like a real idiot standing in the middle of a 7-Eleven, miming licking the fingers of some nonexistent guy.

No wonder he had no friends.

⊙

Beep. Beep. Beep. Beep.

The microwave was going off. It had been going off for the past hour, and it was starting to grate on his nerves. Who cared about fish sticks. Hal reached to turn it off. His arm felt like it was swaddled in cotton. Because it was.

Hal cracked open his eyes. The sheer act of doing so made his eyelids scream in pain. He quickly shut them again. All he'd seen was a bright fluorescent light shining directly into his face, which had hurt, too.

"Hal? Can you hear us?" came an unfamiliar voice. A woman's voice, but not his mom's. Not Siobhan's either. Not that Siobhan was a woman. She was just a girl. A girl who didn't want to be seen in public with him.

Beep. Beep. Beep. Beep.

"He's awake. He likely won't be able to speak for another twelve hours."

"Hal, you stupid, stupid boy." There was his mom's voice. She had that acid bite to her words that told him she was going to cut off his video game access for a week.

"Stupid, but incredibly lucky. Lucky that those looters found him when they did. Lucky that the Hallucigenid that had ambushed him was a juvenile. Weaker than average enzymes in its digestive saliva.

It was probably owing to the hole in his waders that he lost touch with reality. Hallucigenid slime is absorbed quickly through the dermis."

"You hear that, Hal? I'm throwing away those waders for good."

But they were fine. He was fine. Hal tried to shake his head. It was swaddled in cotton, too. Bandages. He was in a hospital bed. In a hospital.

He whimpered.

"We'll up his pain medication now that he's conscious. He has superficial burns, most of them relegated to his face. It's a miracle he's not blind. At least his goggles did their job."

"How long until he can eat solid food?"

"We'll wait until the tissues of his lips are more healed. But I estimate he'll be discharged within a week. Kids his age bounce back fast."

Hal started thrashing. Garbled sounds were coming out of his mouth. Mostly unintelligible. The three women—one internal medicine doctor, one nurse practitioner, and Hal's mother—did their best to soothe him.

"Hal, you need to calm down. Your skin is still healing. If you don't—"

"2 mg Haldol IV. PRN agitation every six hours."

It took five minutes before Hal started thrashing less. Given intravenously, antipsychotics worked fast. He felt the cotton swaddling his limbs go to his brain. He fell into a stupor. Stupor. Stupid. Ha-ha.

While he dozed in and out, Hal's mother reviewed Hal's treatment plan.

"Who is Thom?" the nurse asked Hal's mother before leaving. "He was asking for him. I could barely make it out, but he kept repeating it..."

Hal's mother shook her head. She put a hand on Hal's bandaged head, stroking softly. "Must be one of his friends."

⊙

Herman Melville's Use of Color in the Novel Moby Dick: An Essay

Throughout Moby Dick, an epic novel written by Herman Melville in the year 1851, there is a great deal of emphasis on the color of the whale, which is white. The whiteness of the whale, which is so important that it is even the title of Chapter 42, strongly conveys that the whale is like a ghost, which is haunting to both Captain Ahab as well as Ishmael, the main character of the book. Ahab is obsessed with killing the whale, to the point of seeming insane to the other people on the Pequod, which symbolizes that the pursuit of revenge against perceived evil and a desire to fight back against nihilism is ultimately pointless itself.

In the last paragraph of Chapter 42, Ishmael talks about meaninglessness and how it relates to the color white: "Is it that by its indefiniteness it shadows forth the heartless voids and immensities of the universe, and thus stabs us from behind with the thought of annihilation, when beholding the white depths of the milky way?" (Melville, 200). But then Ishmael goes on to say in the next sentence that white might actually be the absence of color and not a color itself. This speaks to the subjectivity of the experience of meaning, which is common in existentialism, and how that overthinking-process can actually lead to a person going crazy like Ahab, feeling like there is no meaning, no point to anything, and all of us are better off dead. For that reason

Hal lifted his fingers off the keyboard. He threw the brick that was Moby Dick and kicked it to the end of his hospital bed. The book went over the edge, then hit the floor with a loud *thud.*

Fuck homework. He'd missed a week of school, and the second he logged into class again—as if he hadn't almost died—assignments started pouring in. There was another kid in AP English who was behind. Lost a finger or something. The two of them were supposed to trade essays by tomorrow. He still had three and a half paragraphs left to go.

cluecat [9:58]: Send me your outline, Hal. I'll help you

Bangznut [9:59]: tf! u didn't help me on mine (╯°□°)╯︵ ┻━┻

AtlasSniffed [10:00]: favoritism...

Bangznut [10:01]: for hates sake I spit my last breathe at thee!!!!

cluecat [10:01]: Breath*

There came two raps on the door. The nurse and his mother walked in.

"Hal," the nurse said, smiling. Hal could never remember her name. "Are you excited to go home today?"

Way to talk to him like he was eight and not eighteen.

"I could've gone home two days ago," Hal said. He kept typing on his phone. A direct message to Siobhan.

AMercyofCrows [22:21]: thanks

The nurse kept smiling. Her skin was smooth. "Better safe than sorry. Your anti-inflammatories are in this bag. We'll apply the hydrocortisone gel one more time. Then you can get your PPE on and head out while it's still light out."

Hal climbed out of bed. All over his body, his skin was white, the way skin got when he took too long in the shower. A dead layer. It tugged in weird ways every time he moved. He waddled to the bathroom. His mother followed suit.

"It's fine, Mom. I can put it on myself."

"What about your back?" She was already squeezing lime-green gel onto her palm.

"I can reach." Hal shut the door and locked it.

He stared at himself in the bathroom mirror. He turned his head left, right, up, down. The xenopillar's acidic spray had spared his hair, but he still looked like a literal corpse. Pockets of pale skin were ballooning all over his face. When he poked them, he could feel air bubbles inside. There was new skin growing underneath.

He pinched a spot on his cheek with his nails.

A knock on the door startled him. "Hal?" It was his mother's voice, accompanied by jiggling of the door's handle. "You're not picking in there, are you? It'll come off when it's ready."

Five minutes later, Hal waddled out of the bathroom in PPE. There were a few grooves where the xenopillar's mandibles must have tried to get at him. A juvenile. Ha. Hal hoped someone somewhere was spraying it with desiccant so that the ugly bitch would shrivel up like a sun-dried slug.

They took the V-bottom back. Sure enough, the second he finished putting away his gear, his mother wanted to address the video games situation. "Hal. Can we talk?" she asked over the spray of the entry shower.

"No," Hal said automatically. He kept his goggles and face mask on. He was halfway down the hall when he noticed a duffel bag by his mom's door. He spun around. "You're leaving?"

"The lab—"

"They cut your funding. I know. But I thought you weren't going to the one in Bend until February."

Not that it mattered. He'd handled himself fine last spring. This latest close call was just a stupid slip-up. Having a proteomics scientist for a mother meant he'd been raised to be smarter than that.

Hal watched her shake out her hair. After drying off her hands, she walked over. Her crow's feet were more pronounced. That was his fault. Hal shied away from her, but allowed her to gently peel his goggles and face mask off. She clucked her tongue at the hole of dead skin missing on his cheek. "There's an opening now. You know how it is. No notice with these people. You're not going to make me worry when I'm gone, right?"

Hal kept his eyes trained on the floor. "Probably not."

"Yeah, I think you learned your lesson, too." She kissed him. "I'll be here on the weekends. It's temporary until we figure out the grant situation. Call me if you need anything."

"I'll be fine," Hal said.

"We'll see about that. Why don't you check out the kitchen? There's a surprise waiting for you."

She hadn't said anything about the video games. He might as well have been kicked. Hal hung his head. He shuffled into the kitchen. He could barely look at the brand new microwave sitting on the counter top. Its stainless steel gleam made his eyes hurt.

⦿

Xigarette [16:30]: OMggggg just one more hour!!~

Bangznut [16:31]: wait, were we supposed to put the flower thing in the fridge?

cluecat [16:34]: The corsage? Yeah?

Bangznut [16:31]: shiiiiiiiit

Xigarette [16:32]: when's the last time all of us got together in person?

AtlasSniffed [16:32]: ~2 yrs ago. we visited Hal's mom's lab for AP chem proj

Bangznut [16:33]: GUYS. THE FLOWER. THING. IS. BROWN. (>°□°)>

AtlasSniffed [16:33]: gg lol

Xigarette [16:37]: Hal, are u sure you can't come? u're feeling better right?

AtlasSniffed [16:38]: seriously. you don't /need/ a date. i'm going alone too

Steam filled the bathroom. It was a comfortable humidity. Hal had to squeeze past the towers of toilet paper his mother had stored in here to reach the sink. He toweled his hair off, leaned into the mirror, and methodically ran his fingers across his face. The dead skin was finally, finally starting to come loose. Yesterday, he'd peeled it off his arms and chest. Now, it was his face's turn. He found a rough spot on his chin, dug at it with his nail, scratched until he created a hole that he could worm his whole finger inside, and pulled.

He followed the sheet of skin up the contours of his face, over his lips, his nose, his eyes. It came off like cellophane wrap, silently, mostly in one piece.

He didn't know what to do with it at first. It was a triumph; it felt wrong to throw it away. But eventually, standing there, nakedly holding his own skin, he creeped himself out enough to ball it up and chuck it into the trash.

He leaned into the mirror again, close enough that he was fogging up the glass, and methodically ran his fingers across his face. Up his cheeks, across his forehead and eyebrows, down the bridge of his nose. Silky smooth. He couldn't find a single blackhead, not even on either side of his nose. Was this what people meant when they compared stuff to baby skin? Soft, new. He couldn't stop touching it. He'd never been good at growing facial hair. Thank god.

It felt good. He felt good. In the kitchen, he helped himself to his mom's whiskey.

He sank into the couch.

It was too early to sleep, but the Wi-Fi was too shitty to play Val, and Mom wasn't here to do that thing she always did to fix the router. His phone was silent in his pocket. Winter Formal was probably starting now.

Losers.

Hal started picking at the bottom of his foot. He waffled on whether he should go anyway. But by the time he made his decision, it was already over. Signal started blowing up again.

Bangznut [22:01]: NOOOOOO we can't do the afterparty at Xi's she's got like 7 cats
AtlasSniffed [22:01]: sucks to suck.
Xigarette [22:03]: I have benadryl and zyrtec, take ur pick bangz ~_^
cluecat [22:04]: How are you guys not tired yet...
Bangznut [22:05]: if only Oliver hadn't gotten COVID. we could go to his place.
Xigarette [22:03]: girl is that why u were dancing by urself?? why didn't you tell mee TT
cluecat [22:05]: I had a good time!

Hal sat up straight. His fingers were a blur. After shooting off a message, he tossed his phone aside and left to clean up the pigsty he'd been living inside for the past week. He could hear his phone pinging like crazy. He laughed.

AMercyofCrows [22:05]: you all can come here if you want. house is empty
Bangznut [22:05]: POG POG POG
Xigarette [22:06]: Hallllll omg looking forward to seeing you~
cluecat [22:07]: Are we sure? His mom is pretty strict about this stuff
AtlasSniffed [22:07]: what "stuff" are you talking about, Siobhan? don't tell me you were planning on bringing DRUGS to Hal's?
cluecat [22:08]: .....
Xigarette [22:09]: like I said, I have benadryl and zyrtec ~_^

Bangznut [22:10]: I AINT SEEING NO HAT MAN. bringin other fun stuff, see u guyz there —=≡≡(>'-')>

A quarter of an hour later, Hal heard motors spluttering outside. It shouldn't have come as a surprise to him that there were not four people showing up to his place, but seven. Leave it to Bangz to invite a trio of assholes for no discernible reason.

"No way. THIS is Hal Nieffer?"

"Holy crap. You gotta clean your webcam or something, man. This whole time I thought you looked like a fuckin' leper."

"Is it just me or does he look better *after* the werm got to him?"

Hal stared blankly at the two girls and one guy. He didn't recognize them.

Through the open sluice, someone dressed head to toe in gear lumbered into the entry shower. Only Bangz dressed in that garish yellow. He was twirling an air pistol filled with desiccant pellets. It wouldn't kill you, but it could take an eye out. "Alright," Bangz said, voice muffled by his mask. He tapped the closest girl on the head with the air pistol's steel barrel. "Y'all can apologize or swim home. Your pick."

⊙

"ALL MEN live enveloped in whale-lines. ALL are born with HALTERS round their necks; but it is ONLY when caught in the SWIFT, SUDDEN TURN of DEATH, that mortals realize the SILENT, SUBTLE, ever-present perils of LIFE. And if YOU be a philosopher, though seated in the whale-boat, YOU would not at heart feel ONE WHIT more of terror, than though seated before your evening fire with a POKER, and not a harpoon, BY YOUR SIDE—"

"Holy crap, he actually has it memorized..."

Hal watched the group watching Atlas as the guy drunkenly

rocked back and forth on the couch reciting random passages from Moby Dick. He was spilling beer everywhere. They all were.

"You got no chairs in this place, man?" That was Skylar, the guy aspiring to be a doctor. Good luck to him.

"You can sit on Hal's lap," Bangz laughed. He was digging something out of his pocket.

Skylar shot Hal a funny look. If Hal weren't mistaken, it bordered on repulsion. "Get a girl to do it. Then we'll have more room on the couch." He prodded Siobhan with his foot. "You guys are friends. Why don't you take one for the team."

"Don't mess with her," Hal said.

"I'm not messing with her, it's her fuckin' choice—"

Siobhan got up. She walked over, made a face at Hal that Hal couldn't read, and took a seat on his lap. Hal held his breath.

"Aha, I did bring it!" Bangz triumphantly showed off a glass vial. It had a dropper inside, like something you might use for an ear infection. "Y'all ever tried drooz before?"

"It's NOT called drooz," Atlas slurred. "The chemical name is—"

Bangz covered Atlas's mouth with a hand. "No spoilers, babe."

"Drooz?" One of the new girls—her name was either Alee or Lisa, or possibly Alisa—reached for the vial. "Why does that sound familiar?"

"He's referencing the Le Guin short story. The Ones Who Walk Away from Omelas," Siobhan said. When she talked, Hal felt her voice vibrating through his legs. She was precariously balanced. At this rate, she was going to fall off his lap. He thought about steadying her with his hands, and then thought better of it.

"It looks like that shady drug people make milking xenopillars," Skylar said, lip curling.

"MILKING." Xi giggled into her beer.

"Werms gotta be good for something, right?" Bangz snickered. He unscrewed the vial's lid, then squeezed the bulb. He careened around the room. "Who wants to go first?"

Nobody moved. Especially not Hal, whose left hand was on Siobhan's waist now. See? She wasn't going to fall.

"I'll go." To Hal's surprise, it was Siobhan who said it. She slid off Hal's lap, then took the vial from Bangz. Hal watched her lips part as she administered a droplet onto her pink tongue. "How long does it take to work?"

Bangz flashed a toothy smile. "Uhhhh, I don't know. I haven't actually tried it yet—wait, wait, wait, don't freak out! I'm doing it, too. See? Oh fuck, that's nasty."

"Omelas is Salem, O backwards," Atlas mumbled. He stuck his tongue out for Bangz. "Dleifgnirps doesn't sound as good."

Xi ran to the kitchen to wash hers down with milk. Alee and/or Lisa took theirs without a fuss. Skylar had to have his masculinity questioned before he caved.

"How 'bout you, Hal? You joining us or what?"

It was easy for Hal to imagine that the eyedropper had been the one to say it. Inanimate objects talking. Funny that hallucinating came so easily to him. His lap felt cold. "Sure," he said. He held out his hand. "But I'll do it myself."

They were right. It was bitter. Acerbic. Fucking Thom. Bastard couldn't just say it outright.

⊙

How come nothing good in his life ever lasted?

Two weeks of winter break passed in the blink of an eye, and Hal was back to keeping his camera off in class. Garrison, their AP Calc teacher, was rambling about integers or something. Hal scrolled WebMD.

Dermatillomania (Skin Picking Disorder)

A psychological disorder in which a person experiences the impulse to pick at their skin and repeatedly does so, resulting often in scarring and infection.

A person may be at risk for developing skin picking disorder during periods of high stress. Other factors include:

- Low impulse control
- Difficulty regulating emotions
- Sensitivity to skin irregularities
- Co-morbid mental disorders such as anxiety, depression, bipolar, trichotillomania (hair pulling disorder), and obsessive compulsive disorder

Treatment for skin picking disorder ranges from cognitive behavioral therapy and habit reversal therapy to pharmacological solutions such as SSRIs, antipsychotics, and anticonvulsants.

He was almost finished with his two weeks of doxycycline. A wound on his scalp had gotten infected. He was pretty sure the hot compresses were working, but when his lymph nodes started swelling, his mother had dragged him to the express clinic. Annoyingly, the nurse diagnosed him with a mental disorder when he hadn't even asked.

"I was hoping we could get him on Prozac," his mother had said to the nurse.

"We'll start him on 10 mg for a week. We can titrate slowly. It says here he has some metabolic issues."

"I'm not mentally ill," Hal had said. Neither one seemed to hear him.

The bottle of Prozac was sitting on his beside table now. The nurse had impressed it upon him how important it was that he stop taking it immediately if he developed suicidal thoughts. The only thing he noticed was that it was harder than usual to masturbate.

There was a smooth bald spot on his scalp now where the infection was healing. Hal rubbed it a few times, then stopped. How fucking stupid would that be if he gave himself a hair-pulling problem on top of everything.

He checked Signal. No new messages. Just one he had sent to Siobhan a day ago, unread.

AMercyofCrows [7:13]: hey. can we talk about what happened

Hal dropped his head into his hands.

The group chat was dead, too. Not a peep even from Bangz. At least they would all be graduating soon. It was just high school. All friend groups fell apart one way or another.

His bald spot itched. He needed to do something with his hands, so he cleaned his room by way of sweeping the pile of scabs and dead skin off his desk onto the floor. Then, feeling disgusting, he grabbed the vacuum and did some actual cleaning.

Medication was one thing, but like hell he was going to get a therapist. He was supposed to go up to 20 mg of the Prozac tonight. It would fix him.

Except it didn't. Thank god his mom kept having to pull overtime in Bend, or else seeing him, she'd gorilla glue rubber mittens onto his fingers. Hal dug his old anti-inflammatories out of the medicine cabinet and slathered them over his face. It burned like hell. He was so fucking stupid. It was one spot, and he couldn't leave it alone. Only one positive had come out of getting slimed in that 7-Eleven, and he'd squandered it. Skylar was right. He looked like a leper. No wonder girls like Siobhan wanted nothing to do with him.

I'm sorry, he typed. He deleted it without sending it to her.

There were frozen fish sticks in the garage freezer, like always. Beside the box was a frozen pack of chicken thighs. His mom liked to bake them with rosemary. He kept telling her he didn't like rosemary. He had a gene that made them taste like pine needles.

Later, his mom would ask him what happened to those chicken thighs she'd saved. He'd tell her he cooked them in the microwave.

It wasn't like him to lie. But he'd always been quick to adapt.

⊙

Hal brought night-vision goggles this time. His eyesight was garbage without his glasses, but NODs came with a diopter you could adjust. The sign on the 7-Eleven's door still looked blurry even when he was standing a foot away from it, but it was better than fumbling around with a flashlight, especially when he needed both hands to use a rifle.

CLOSED INDEFINITELY

Slimy glass crunched underfoot. Since shoving Dr. Scholl's inserts into his new waders, they weren't giving him blisters anymore. Still weren't as comfortable as the old ones, though. The old ones he kept as a reminder to not be fucking stupid.

One foot. *Plip.*

Five feet. *Plip.*

Twenty-something feet. *Plip.*

No reactivity from the pebbles, so that meant the coast was clear, right?

Hal snorted. Sure.

He wasn't alone in here. Sometimes you could just tell.

Compared to the last time he'd been here, the 7-Eleven actually looked like a place you could get slimed at. The passing months had not been kind to the building. The owners had given up on trying to put it back together after the water levels rose again. The pump that normally kept water away from the door was out of commission, so the place was flooded to his ankles. Rotting food, junky appliances, and other trash swirled around him like a noxious cocktail.

Hal waded in quietly. Something hissed a few aisles down.

He readied his rifle. Xenopillars hissed only when they were scared, aggro, mating, or injured. Basically, the only time you didn't hear a xenopillar was when it was right on top of you.

Which meant whatever it was doing had nothing to do with him.

He waded past the chip aisle. Then the soda aisle. A clump of hair drifted past him. Or maybe it was the head of a Swiffer.

More hissing.

He could leave now. The exit was only six feet away. He could back up just as quietly. But if he left now, he would be back home in about fifteen minutes, and Siobhan probably hadn't messaged him back, and he would probably explode or kill himself if he let himself double-text her like Reddit kept telling him not to.

That was probably why he didn't feel a lick of regret when he rounded the last aisle and came face to face with three xenopillars.

Saying there were three of them was pushing it, though. More like two-and-a-half. The two in the armored phase were about the size of ponies—average for that phase—meaning they were at least three years old. They'd get spines during their fourth year if they survived that long, which was actually becoming less and less a rarity. The third was between them, half their size, fat and white like a maggot. A juvenile.

Fucking Thom.

It was Thom who was doing all the hissing. No doubt owing to the fact that the bigger duo had bitten off two of his nubby legs. Both were rearing with their mandibles out in that pose xenopillars did when they were about to spit acid. Cannibalism wasn't uncommon between werms. As Atlas might say, *sucks to suck.*

Hal fired two bullets. Both hit their mark, crushing through armored plating. The two larger xenopillars crumpled, spewing acid and blood. He really was a good shot.

Thom kept hissing and, when Hal stepped closer, ejected a few ropes of watery slime at him. They coated Hal's chest and instantly hardened. A bit of twisting and they cracked apart easily.

"You're out of juice, Thom," he said.

Predictably, Thom replied with more hissing.

Hal opened his bag. He fished out the chicken thighs, peeled off the cellophane wrap—not easy to do with gloves on—and palmed one. Skinless. It had defrosted on the way over. "Same age as me, huh? Thom, you fucking liar. You're barely two."

"*Sssstthhhssss*," said Thom.

It was way easier talking to a xenopillar than to a person. Xenopillars were good listeners. They didn't get upset when you screamed "fuck you, fuck you, fuck you, fuck you, fuck you" at them.

Hal tossed the chicken thigh. It splatted on Thom's face. Fine, xenopillars didn't have faces. It splatted between his slime papillae.

When the chicken thigh plopped into the water, Thom recoiled. His fat maggoty body scrunched up as he tried to back into a rusty shelving unit. Fucking stupid werm didn't even know when it was being offered a free meal.

Hal imagined killing it with desiccant. Nice and slow.

His lip curled. He took the yellow styrofoam plate, peeled off the rest of the plastic, and, wading closer, held the chicken thighs up to Thom's mouth. Werms had an 'o' shaped mouth. It was used to create a suction when feeding, because werms were like spiders in that they digested their food extra-orally. Thom's 'o' gently brushed the surface of the raw chicken. Acidic digestive saliva started oozing out of it.

Hal took a glass vial out of his pocket. He collected as much saliva as he could, until it overflowed the vial. He then capped it.

"You help me, I help you," Hal said.

Thom was too busy drooling over chicken thighs to hiss. No talking at the dinner table. Ha-ha.

Thirty seconds passed.

The 7-Eleven was silent, save for the sound of Thom's salivary glands pumping fluid. Black water swirled around Hal's waders. Something floated past. Just the head of a Swiffer after all.

He should have left. He'd gotten what he needed. But instead, Hal just stood there and watched, transfixed, as the raw chicken started bubbling. Thom's pink mouth glistened with digestive fluid. It was translucent, milky. It reminded him of the way his own cum had stained Siobhan's lips.

⊙

In addition to being a hallucinogenic, xenopillar slime could double as an aphrodisiac. It depended on how lucky you were. Something about their reproductive cycle. Their friend group had to learn that the hard way. Hal wasn't sure if the same applied to xenopillar saliva, but he would quickly find out.

"F-fuck... fuck, fuck..." He worked his dick, eyes rolling into the back of his head. His face burned—not from shame; he just hadn't diluted the xenopillar acid enough—but every stroke he administered to himself made him feel like his whole body was turning into one giant reproductive organ getting shoved into a girl's pussy.

Not just any girl's.

He came four times in the span of fifteen minutes. The fourth time, nothing even came out. *You're out of juice,* he remembered telling Thom. Karma's a bitch.

After that, he lay in bed, naked from the waist down, splayed out like a starfish, zoning out at the ceiling which was throbbing with a million colors like a TV station glitching the fuck out. His nerves tingled. Breathing felt good. His bedsheets felt so fucking good. And

FUCK, he was hard again. Could a person die from ejaculating too many times? Maybe he should apologize to Siobhan instead of touching himself. That would be the normal thing to do. Normal was good. It was also necessary to balance out the fact that he had abnormally, purposefully slathered his face with werm saliva less than an hour ago, and was now abnormally, purposefully pumping himself to life while imagining how fucking amazing Siobhan's voice would sound in his ear right about now—

"I wouldn't do that if I were you," a voice said.

Hal dropped his phone and his dick at the same time. He blinked.

Sitting across from him in his own computer chair, arms crossed, was a guy. White hair, red eyes. It was Thom. Only he wasn't wearing the green 7-Eleven polo anymore. He was wearing one of Hal's oversized hoodies.

"You're not... you're not..." Hal's voice came out ragged.

"Don't tell me. I'm not supposed to be in here?" Thom had picked up a stack of AP Gov flashcards and was thumbing through them. "Door was unlocked. I let myself in."

But they didn't have a door. They had a sluice gate. "You're not real," Hal said, composing himself.

"I mean, you have retinas, don't you? Don't I look pretty real?" Thom winked.

Charming. Not.

"Hallucigenid slime is absorbed quickly through the dermis" yadda yadda medical jargon flashback. Hal's dermis was covered in the stuff, a nice thin layer from his forehead down to his chin, and his dick hanging out was solid evidence of that. Thom wasn't wrong, though. He looked real. Sounded real. The experience was *multimodal.* From his spot slumped in bed, Hal could see the fine hairs on the backs of Thom's fingers as he thumbed through his flashcards. Thom's lips were pink, the right corner hooked in a mischievous smile. There was a hole in the sleeve of the hoodie he had on. Hal remembered getting it snagged on some chain link

fencing the first time he snuck into the clearing behind the swimming pool.

Or had he?

His eyelids sank. His dick pulsed. Thom lifted an eyebrow.

"Well, you're clearly busy, so I'll quit teasing you. I just wanted to give you a bit of advice. That girl you were about to call? Don't. Give her some time to come around." Thom grunted as he stood up.

Hal felt another wave of euphoria crest over him. He whimpered.

"Really, now." Sighing, Thom walked over and petted the top of Hal's head. "Your mom just got home, by the way. You might want to get your act together. Peace, kid."

Hal blinked, and Thom was gone.

A gentle knock sounded on the door. "Hal? Are you on the phone still?"

It took a minute for Hal to wrestle pants on. He wasn't sober by any means, evidenced by the fact that he paused to rub his dick a few more times. He could only pray his mom would guess he broke into her whiskey stores again. "Yeah, just finished VCing Bangz." He leaned against the doorframe so his knees wouldn't give in. "What's up."

His mother's eyes immediately homed in on his face. "Is that a facial mask?"

"Yeah. Xi lent me some of hers. How was work?"

She took the bait instantly. "Great. Really, great." Her hands were moving a lot, which meant she was excited. "I've mentioned hydrolases to you before... Complex cocktail of digestive enzymes in Hallucigenid saliva that breaks down the extracellular matrix... Water causes the dissolution of disulfide-bonded complexes, yes, but the lab just made a real breakthrough... Re-solubilized Hallucigenid slime has structural proteins which may be useful for not only breaking down tissue, but *repairing* it."

"Uh-huh," Hal said. He smiled.

His mother had always said his smile was infectious. She must have been onto something, because she started to smile, too. Her eyes crinkled. Maybe crow's feet meant you were happy. "It's all going right over your head, isn't it, hon?"

"A little," Hal said. He squeezed past her. "Need to use the bathroom."

"Someone's in a good mood" was the last thing he heard her say before he slammed the bathroom door behind him.

He exploded in his pants even before he managed to get his underwear off. Panting, slumped over the sink, he eyed his reflection in the mirror. He looked pretty good, actually. The slime mask covered a lot of his scars. You couldn't tell from the outside how much it tingled.

"Your mom's a smart cookie," a voice said.

Hal's eyes slid to the right. Thom was sitting on the closed toilet lid. He had a pensive look.

"Thought you were leaving," Hal gurgled. He puddled to his knees.

"Yeah, I was." Thom clucked his tongue. He got down beside Hal, then petted his hair again. "But you look like you could use some help."

A hallucination sucked him off better than his own real-life crush had. When it was over, Hal passed out on the tiled bathroom floor. Normal was good. Necessary, even. But abnormal was a lot more memorable.

⊙

This was the part Hal looked forward to the most.

Sometimes, it was fun to start under his ear. He could nestle his middle finger into the hollow right behind his detached lobe and rub, rub, rub until he got an edge lifted. Starting with that edge, he would take his time tracing his jawline, using his finger—he liked to switch up which—like a letter opener, lifting his skin off like a mask.

It wasn't good if it rolled up too early. The better technique was to add a second hand and fan his fingers out, walking them like spider legs up his cheeks. If it came off in chunks, that was fine. It just meant he would have to spend a bit more time in front of the bathroom mirror peeling it off in little strips, making sure that there was no raised demarcation between the old and the new. There was always cleanup to do around the corners of his eyes and around his philtrum, which he was happy to indulge. *Indulge.* That was the word. But the way he saw it, it wasn't all that different from the preening birds did.

Morning rituals were different for everyone. So what if the best part of Hal's day was getting to peel his own dead skin off?

"You know, your face would heal better if you stopped picking at it all day."

That was Thom speaking. He was in Hal's bed reading a book. Hal ignored him. He finished toweling off his hair and sat down at his desk. Teach was still rambling about integers.

Sometimes, even after he was sure the hallucinogenic was out of his system, Hal saw Thom like this. He Googled schizophrenia, but didn't think it was applicable, so he stopped Googling altogether. Not like it mattered. He knew Thom wasn't real. He had both feet firmly anchored in reality. It was just a necessary side effect. Somatic.

"This book is wild," Thom said. "Can I read you this part?"

Hal didn't turn around. "Shut up. I'm trying to take a quiz."

"Maybe I can help. I'm decent at math. Is it derivative stuff?"

Hal didn't answer. Ten minutes later, he turned in his quiz. Seven out of ten. Good enough.

"Alright, now that you're done," Thom said, sidling to the edge of Hal's mattress. He cleared his throat and extended a hand as if he were going to recite Hamlet. "'Squeeze! squeeze! squeeze! all the morning long; I squeezed that sperm till I myself almost melted into it; I squeezed that sperm till a strange sort of insanity came over me;

and I found myself unwittingly squeezing my co-laborers' hands in it, mistaking their hands for the gentle globules—'"

"Enough."

"Sound familiar?" Thom's voice was dripping with smarm. "You, like Ishmael, also enjoy it when someone squeezes your—"

Signal pinged. Then it pinged again. And again.

Actually, it was ringing. Hal's heart began to thump wildly.

He was receiving a call from Siobhan.

"Hal." Her voice was shy, featherlight. Exactly what Hal had been craving. She wasn't mad at him. She wouldn't be talking to him if she were mad at him. "I wanted to apologize... for giving you the cold shoulder this past week. I... after what we did. What we all did. I just needed time to process it. I want to thank you for giving me that time, Hal."

Thanking him? Was she going to cut him off for good? Hal's hands were shaking. *I'm sorry, I'm sorry, I'm sorry* was all he wanted to say. How could he make it sound genuine? It was genuine. It was so genuine he thought he might be sick.

"It's fine. I needed time, too," was what he forced himself to say. Nice and even.

"We're so stupid, aren't we? Jesus. I really can't wait until we graduate. It's just a few months from now."

"Yeah. Crazy."

"What do you think we should do about the group chat? I hate how quiet it is. I don't want to lose any of you guys as friends. I don't think Gray would want that."

"Gray would have been smart enough not to eat werm slime."

That got Siobhan to laugh. Hal squeezed his hand into a fist, so tight his knuckles turned white. "There's a funny meme I could post," he said.

"Oh! That's a good idea. Post it now. I'll like it, and I'll tell Xi to like it, too."

"What about Bangz and Atlas?"

"Between you and me..." Siobhan giggled. It was like her breath was tickling Hal's eardrum. Or maybe it was the xenopillar acid he'd just applied starting to kick in. "Actually, never mind. I'll tell you later. Go ahead and send the meme. I'll wait a few minutes before I like it so it's not too obvious we were talking."

"Is it bad if we're talking?" Hal ventured. He bit his tongue immediately after.

Siobhan was silent for a moment. "No, I... Oh, sorry. One sec. Mom is asking me something. Can I call you back later?"

Fucking hell. Fucking stupid fucking hell. I need to die. "Sure," Hal said. "I should be paying attention to class anyway."

"Okay! Talk later!" Beep.

Hal threw his phone across the room. He walked over to his bed and flung himself face down onto the mattress. Thom, who had clearly been eavesdropping, rolled out of the way just in time not to be crushed. Which would make sense only if he weren't a total figment of Hal's imagination.

"Kid. It's just one girl. There're a million fish in the sea."

Hal moaned into his pillow. It was a half-emotionally-tormented-half-sexual kind of moan. His dick was throbbing again. He wouldn't touch it. Not today.

"C'mon." Thom's voice tickled Hal's eardrum. A hand slid into his underwear. "I know what'll make you feel better."

He was right, in that older brother way. Gross. Ha-ha.

"You're not real," Hal said. He let the colors on the ceiling tickle his eyeballs and began working his hips. The high always took twenty-two minutes to really get started. He was soaring. It was so fucking natural. Just an animal sort of thing.

Thom laughed, and Hal, gasping, came all over himself, fountains of endless cum. "Kid, you can't handle real," Thom said, and their mouths overlapped.

⊙

me 5 years ago: labubu dubai chocolate love island <3
me now: sandy. that's not the worm. that's his tongue.
Xigarette [11:17]: hhhhhh
AMercyofCrows [11:19]: i don't get it
cluecat [11:21]: That's probably for the best
Bangznut [11:24]: HAHAHAHAHAHAH WAIT LOOK AT THIS ONE
Bangznut [11:24]:
anti-maskers during COVID: [stock photo of a guy thumbs-up-ing the camera]
anti-maskers now: [graphic photo of a human corpse being eaten by a Hallucigenid]
Xigarette [11:24]: stawppppp rofl
AtlasSniffed [11:25]: darwinism…
cluecat [11:21]: Can we spoiler that stuff please? ;;

Hearing a series of knocks on his door, Hal glanced up from his phone. The handle jiggled. It was locked. Obviously.

"Busy!" he yelled. He minimized his Excel spreadsheet.

"Hal, your senior photos just came in," his mom said through the door. "Take a look. They turned out really well."

Was that sniffling? Probably not. His mom wasn't the emotional type. The only time he ever saw her cry was when she was cutting onions.

He opened the door. Her eyes were red. *Definitely* onions. She held up a square photo of him, already framed. He was sitting, leaned over with his arms dangling over his lanky legs, smiling up at the camera. He remembered the photographer had taught him a trick for getting that smile. *Just imagine the most embarrassing moment of your life.* Not like it was hard to pick. Dappled sunlight filtered in through the maple trees behind him. The angle of the photo was taken in such a way that you couldn't see the fields of swampland surrounding them.

"I'm proud of you, hon," she said. She hugged him.

Yeah, he was proud of himself, too. The xenopillar slime was doing wonders for his face. No matter how raw and bloody he scratched himself up, the next morning he'd peel and be good as new. Sayonara, finger mittens.

"Don't hang it up," Hal told her, handing back the photo. In the kitchen, he dished up a bowl of fried rice. Sure enough, it had onions.

His mom chuckled. "Hang it up? I'm taking it with me to Bend."

Just don't show it to anyone, he wanted to say. Instead, he asked, "What time are you leaving?"

"Good question. The V-bottom's motor is acting up again. I might need to run to Home Depot first. Sun's going down, though. Dinner took longer than I thought."

"You can still make it if you leave now," Hal said casually.

Not casually enough, judging by the suspicious look she gave him. *Shit.* "You're that eager to get me out of the house?" she asked, quirking a brow. "Don't think I don't know what's been happening here while I'm gone, Hal Nieffer."

"Sharp as a tack, that woman," said Thom. He'd appeared in the kitchen and was helping himself to Hal's bowl of fried rice. He was naked, aside from wearing Hal's underwear.

Hal forced himself to look his mom in the eye instead of at the outline of Thom's dick. "Don't know what you're talking about," he mumbled.

It wasn't like him to lie. Look, he wasn't even good at it.

"You might legally be an adult, Hal, but you're still living in my house. Substance abuse isn't something to mess around with." His mother's arms were akimbo. Coupled with her wild hair, it had the effect of making her look bigger than she really was. In reality, Hal dwarfed her in height. Everyone always said he was a tall kid. "It stops here. Do I make myself clear?"

"We could kill her," Thom suggested.

"No," said Hal.

"No?" His mom sounded more bewildered than angry. Maybe she was too tired to get angry at him anymore. When he was a kid, she used to throw things. When had that stopped? "Go ahead and check the cupboard. You know the one I'm talking about."

He followed her line of sight and opened the cupboard above the microwave. There was nothing in it. Definitely not his stash of home-baked xenopillar slime exfoliant, which he kept under the bathroom sink. Hidden in plain sight.

"Okay," he said.

"I dumped it all down the sink. Every last drop. These aren't pre-Hallucigenid times. Whiskey isn't cheap. But I'm not going to stand by and watch you turn into an alcoholic." His mom stepped closer. She put a hand on his arm. "I love you. You know that, right?"

"Yeah," Hal said.

He let her hug him. She sniffled into his shoulder. Maybe it wasn't onions after all. Maybe it was just him being a piece of shit.

He waited until she was out of the house before re-opening his Excel spreadsheet. He had a list of the different ratios he was experimentally diluting Thom's saliva with to reduce the harsh acidity, and a list of skincare products he had tried, to varying levels of success. The acid was drying out his skin, so he needed something hydrating. A serum with 1.5% hyaluronic acid, followed by moisturizer and jojoba oil, was his current regimen. That, and werm spit.

"Shit," Hal said, vial in hand.

Thom poked his head into the bathroom. "All good in here?" he asked.

Hal glanced at the mirror. Now Thom really *was* naked. *Tu casa es mi casa,* as he liked to say. It was the one thing he claimed to remember from Spanish class. Thom was a better liar than Hal was, but only by about 2 percent.

"Put your dick away." Hal tried to shut the door, but it wouldn't close. Thom's foot was in the way.

Multimodal was getting to be a real pain in the ass.

"You can call yours a dick, but you gotta call mine a cock. Got it?" Thom wriggled into the bathroom. When he saw the glass vial Hal was fussing with, he plucked it out of Hal's hand and inspected it in the light. "Doesn't look like you got much left in here."

"It's empty."

Thom's eyes sparkled. If he had a tail, it would be wagging. "Does that mean—"

He dogged Hal down the hall and into the kitchen. When Hal wrestled a whole rotisserie chicken into his backpack, Thom did a double-take. "That whole thing for me? But what are you going to eat tomorrow?"

"I'll figure something out," Hal said.

"Let me cook for you sometime. It's the least I can do."

Hearing this, Hal nearly lost his balance. His waders were half on. "The least you can do *for what?*"

Thom laughed. He petted Hal's head. He'd learned fast—too fast—that Hal liked it when his fingers raked up his nape, tugging gently on his hair. Hal closed his eyes and let it happen. Thom's words bothered him a lot less than they should have.

"You saved my life, Hal. Did you think I'd forget?"

⊙

Of course Hal wouldn't forget that. Not when he visited Thom every other day to check how his nubby legs were healing. It wouldn't do if his acid dealer got necrosis and went belly up.

Who could have guessed anti-inflammatories would work on xenopillars, too.

Slimy glass crunched underfoot.

Sunsets were really something to behold these days. Orange light slanted in through the smashed windows. The abandoned 7-Eleven had become a second home of sorts. Hal had jerry-rigged the sump pump by the door so it was no longer flooded inside. Granted, when it rained, that all went out the window, but the forecast said clear skies for the week. Technically, that gave the upper hand to the xenopillars, but being around Thom had made Hal a lot more confident about killing them. Xenopillars were so pathetic.

"Fucking hell, Thom, it's me!" Hal shouted.

Too late. He was coated head to toe in Thom's rapidly hardening "silly string of death."

"*Sssstthhhssss*," said Thom.

Did xenopillars know how to apologize? The answer, obviously, was no. Hal told Thom to stand back, which did absolutely nothing because Thom was an unintelligent bug. "If you get desiccant on you, that's your fault," Hal said. He managed to unclip his canister, a real feat given that his limbs were encased in slime, and started misting himself. When a droplet of desiccant landed on Thom's face, Thom scrambled away, hissing like a slice of bacon.

"Getting around fine with only fourteen legs instead of sixteen," Hal noted. Once his limbs were free again, he pointed at the floor. "Come. Here."

Again, unintelligent bug. Hal had to bring the rotisserie chicken out to get Thom's attention. As soon as Thom was at his feet oozing over the seasoned meat—he really didn't give a shit whether it was cooked or not, so far as Hal could tell—Hal did his usual sample collection.

Then, he did something he really fucking shouldn't have learned how to do.

He reached out a gloved hand and stroked Thom's back. The same way you'd pet a cat. Xenopillars didn't like it when you went the other way. So weird. It wasn't as if they had fur.

"*Ssssttthhhsssssssssss*," said Thom.

Hal rubbed the rubbery plates along Thom's spine. Not spine.

Thom was an invertebrate. "You're getting your armor in already. I guess I was wrong about your age. Birthday's coming up, huh."

Thom hissed louder. He was sucking on the rotisserie chicken now, rabidly, the way a horny teen might suck on a girl's tits. Or a guy's. It didn't actually matter which when you thought about it.

Thom's body was squishy. Hal gently kneaded it. Had Siobhan's tits been this soft? They hadn't actually taken their clothes off that night. There was no p-in-v action. That meant he was a virgin still. Blowjobs were only third base.

"Thom," Hal said. He could feel the werm pressing into his thigh. The sound of chicken melting was like a gooey song in his ears. Drippy. Wet. "I really didn't like what you said earlier. About killing my mom."

"C'mon. I was just teasing, kid. You know how I am."

Hal turned, following the voice. Sitting at a wooden dining table in the center of the 7-Eleven was Thom. Human Thom. Wearing a fancy button-up, tie, and slacks.

He'd never hallucinated about Thom next to xenopillar Thom. Come to think of it, where did xenopillar Thom go?

"You always wanted to know what the older kids were doing behind that swimming pool. Well, what do you think?" Thom asked. He motioned to the walls covered in ivy.

And there it was. The whiteboard he had always dreamed about. There was nothing written on it. Not yet.

"How is this possible?" Hal asked.

Thom clucked his tongue. "It's like you always say. It's not real. Look." He wiggled a finger.

Hal looked down at his own hand. His left glove, the one that had been holding the vial collecting acid, had a hole eaten where his ring finger was. Used to be. Acid didn't discriminate between synthetic rubber and skin. You could see the bone. There was a lot of blood, but it didn't hurt.

"Oh," Hal said.

"You noticed it too, right? You kept having to dilute me more and more. I guess you forgot, huh. Sorry. I should have been more transparent. But I was hoping..."

Thom had a knife and fork in his hands now. He was sawing off a piece of chicken, which sat on a plate in front of him. He popped it, bones and all, into his mouth. A piece of rosemary stuck to his pink bottom lip.

"Would it be gross if we kissed?"

"Yeah," said Hal. The sunlight was burning his eyes. "It would be really fucking gross."

"But you sort of like gross, don't you."

Hal didn't answer. He felt like he was butt naked. He pawed his clothes. Nope, still geared up, minus the effed up glove. Wow, it was a straight-up skeletal finger now. He'd forgotten there was a skeleton inside of him. That was one big major difference between him and Thom.

Once, in junior year biology, they had to dissect xenopillar nymphs.

The nymphs were the size of your forearm.

Here were the jaw-blades and here were the denticles. And here were the salivary glands and digestive tract. They discovered werms had penises. Or was the word *spermatophore* more appropriate? There was nothing appropriate about musing about the *ejaculatory apparatus* of werms. That apparatus being the *intromittent organ* that a sexually receptive boy werm would press against a sexually receptive girl werm's opening.

"Don't overthink it, Hal. Come. Here." Thom winked.

Hal whimpered.

His feet were moving on their own. He sat down on Thom's lap, the spot where Thom was patting. He felt like he was going to fall off until Thom settled a hand on his waist. "We'll take it slow. Is there a zipper on this thing?"

"Take what slow?" Hal asked. He asked, but he knew.

"Oh, I see. It comes off all in one go. I can help with that. Hold still," Thom soothed. His moist tongue darted out and Hal could smell that burning rubber smell that meant his gear was starting to break down. This was bad bad bad bad bad bad super bad, Hal thought. His heart was hammering like crazy. Thom's hands gently sought his skin. His cool fingers trailed lower and lower and reached the small of Hal's back.

"I'm scared, Thom," Hal said. His teeth were chattering.

"You don't trust me?"

"Oh, fuck. F-f-fuck."

Exactly twenty-two minutes must have passed. Substance abuse wasn't something to play around with. None of Mom's smart genes had gone to him. It wasn't fair he was born stupid.

Hal looked down. Between his legs—his waders were still on, thank god—was Thom's dick. Cock. It looked just like Hal's own dick/cock. It was a human cock. Rigid, veiny, its slit leaking fluid. The foreskin was starting to pull back. He couldn't stop staring at it.

What if Thom's precum was acidic, too? What if it melted him from the inside? What kind of ultra fucked up question was that? Hal wasn't getting anywhere near Thom's precum.

"I just want you to touch me, Hal. Just touch me a little bit, and then we can stop."

He didn't need to be told that. He already *was* touching Thom. Slippery. These gloves were so stupidly, unnecessarily thick. He couldn't feel it pulsing like he was supposed to. Weirdly, his eyeballs could feel it, but his hands were missing out.

"Thom. I think... I think we're gonna—"

"Yeah, you're getting there, kid. You're almost ready for me."

"What's... what's actually happening?"

Thom hummed. "I'm not sure you want to know the answer to that."

There was a heartbeat pounding against Hal's back. Hal wanted so badly to believe that it was a human heart. It was normal to want sex, human to human. He flung his head back and helped Thom help him shuck his waders off.

Maybe he was still at home in bed. Just a messed-up fantasy.

A pair of hands coaxed Hal's legs open. Thom's cock was like a fleshy pole rubbing against his sac. For a second, Hal couldn't see anything past that kaleidoscope of fireworks. When Thom wrapped a hand around him and started rhythmically pulling him off, each motion was accompanied by a sucking sound, more deafening than was normal.

Thom nuzzled his nape. "You look cute like this."

It was nice being called cute.

Hal's mouth was slack. He couldn't respond. Splayed out on Thom's lap, he'd gone limp. Something was prodding, lapping against his buttocks, dipping into the crevice there. It made no sense. Thom's cock was still between his thighs, right there where he could see it, intoxicatingly slippery.

"Okay, I think I understand," Thom said.

Sometimes, there was hardly a distinction between hallucination and memory.

"Class," said some disembodied biology teacher's voice. "Can someone tell me what these are?"

Snickers rippled through the classroom. Hal sat in the back. He tried to laugh with them and failed. Some kid offered the word *hentai helpers*. Not especially creative.

And sometimes, reality broke through.

He was on the floor, cold linoleum against his bare back. Foam in the corner of his mouth. Something soft undulating on top of him. Hissing.

No, Hal thought. He convulsed as a wave of euphoria zinged across his nerves. The prodding thing took advantage of his relaxing muscles and slipped inside. Once it entered, it gained confidence, reaching deeper and deeper, molding to him like liquid. *No, no, no, maybe, yes, maybe, no, yes, yes, yes, yes, please, God, yes.*

"I'm glad I have one of these," Thom moaned. His eyelids

fluttered. He was bucking. "We're not that incompatible. It's not what we were built for, but we make do."

Hal could feel himself pulsing. It wouldn't stop. Each contraction wrenched an animal sound out of him. That was his voice bouncing off the walls.

What if someone heard him? They could shoot him in the face for all he cared.

"F-fuck me, Thom. Fuck me, fuck me, fuck me, *fuck me*—"

"Yeah, I think"—Thom's voice cracked; he sank deeper into Hal's channel—"think I'll keep doing you like this. I love how you feel, Hal. You make sense now. I kept thinking I could get to you. I was right."

Coming.

"I'm gonna give you something, Hal. A little keepsake."

Coming.

"I hope you understand."

Coming.

The thing inside him was pumping fluid. He could feel it. And Thom's voice made it so much better: "Kid, I'm sorry, but you're never going to be the same—"

"HAL, WHAT THE *FUCK.*"

⊙

How come nothing good in his life ever lasted?

That voice was like a hammer crushing Hal's skull. It made all the intoxicant in his veins instantly dry up. Hal sobered up for a fleeting moment and saw, standing in the doorway of his 7-Eleven, a person.

Who wore garish yellow again? It was on the tip of Hal's tongue.

"Oh. Hey, Bangz..."

The little bit you could see of Bangz's face was ashen. The sclera of his eyes were visible through his goggles. An expression like that, you might seriously be able to convince yourself he (Bangz) was the one caught fucking a werm and not the other way around.

You couldn't blame him though. It felt good. If people knew, they'd be fucking werms left and right.

Hal's eyes drifted south. How nice. His waders were still in one piece. Only problem was, they were on the floor instead of on him like they should be. Crumpled up like dead skin.

Maybe after today, he'd go home, hide out in the bathroom, and peel himself clean to the bone.

Hal tried to stand. Something slid out of him, the feeling so exquisite that he felt himself coming again. It was a weak spurt. Oops. His next senior photos, he was guaranteed to have the best smile ever.

"Hal. Hal. Come here. Please," Bangz said.

His voice was surprisingly gentle. Maybe he wasn't disgusted? Did he want to join? He was extending a hand towards Hal. His other hand was raising that dinky air pistol.

Bangz was too scared to carry a real gun. It was a gun that had killed his dad, see. Xenopillars weren't the only thing you had to watch out for.

People were animals, too.

"It was Thom's idea," Hal gurgled. He slipped and fell to his knees. Black fluid trickled down the insides of his thighs. "Don't tell anyone, 'kay?"

"I won't tell. Christ, Hal. Hal."

What a relief. Bangz was such a good friend. Better than Siobhan. "My finger hurts," Hal said. He held it up. No more skeleton. It was just a stump. He and Thom were matching now. Ha-ha.

Bangz froze. He was always posting graphic shit in the group chat. It shouldn't have scared him *that* bad. It would grow back, right? Or was that just a starfish thing?

Hal shivered pleasantly. A soft white appendage had wrapped around his middle, drawing him against a soft white body. Oh, Thom. You know how he is.

"Hal, get the fuck down!" Bangz screamed. He raised the air pistol.

Have you ever seen desiccant BBs get stopped midair by a rope of slime? It's quite the image.

"Hal! Hal! The desiccant! Throw it to me!" It was a command first. Then a plea.

That stuff might hurt Thom, though. Thom wasn't a bad guy. He would introduce him and Bangz, and they would get along, and Bangz would ask Hal if it was okay to fuck Thom too, and Hal would say "sure, what are friends for?" But first, a nap.

Hal closed his eyes. When he opened them again, he was lying on his side, staring at a pile of melted meat.

"Why'd you follow me, Bangz?" Hal asked.

Thom sighed. "He was worried about you, I guess." He licked his fingers. "You hungry, Hal? I made dinner."

"I'm okay," Hal said. He kept laying there. The melted meat was smiling at him. So many teeth. Usually you couldn't see all of them at once like this. It was helpful when there wasn't any skin left to hide them.

"*Sssstthhhssss*," said Thom. *Suit yourself. More for me.*

⊙

Once, there had been six of them.

You didn't bury people in Springfield. Not unless you wanted to risk a dead body spontaneously un-burying itself and washing up on some riverbank, bloated with xenopillar larva. It was hard to tell where and when water levels would rise. Cremation wasn't good for the environment. But besides that, you needed a body to cremate in the first place. Given enough time, xenopillar acid could dissolve bone. Even teeth.

The cemetery was in the heart of town. It was easy to get to. It had rows and rows of columbarium walls, which generally housed whatever items you wanted to remember a person by. Each niche had a memorial plaque on it with a name and a quote.

The six of them picked out their quotes in middle school, the day it occurred to them that shit was bad and wasn't getting better. Since then, only Bangz's had stayed the same.

In heaven, all the interesting people are missing.

Just wanna let this story go~

The way to see how beautiful the earth is, is to see it as the moon. The way to see how beautiful life is, is from the vantage point of death.

IM FREEEEEE!!!!!!!! WORST EXPERIENCE OF MY FUCKING LIFE

Omnia mors aequat.

Gray's memorial plaque was the first to see its quote carved into being. It was from an old-as-dirt video game she'd been obsessed with. When she was still alive, you rarely got to make eye contact with her because of that emulator she was glued to all day every day. Hal had visited her enough times over the last four years that he had it memorized.

When on your way out
Be sure to say goodnight
Then shut the door tight.

You didn't get used to burying friends. Burying classmates, sure. But never friends.

Now, it was just the four of them.

"Atlas still can't come. I went to the clinic to see him this morning. He just keeps saying Bangz isn't dead. Over and over. Something about a coffin. They have him on suicide watch."

Siobhan said it more to herself than anyone else. Xi was sobbing, snot getting all over her mask. Hal stared unblinkingly at Bangz's plaque.

There was nothing written on it. Not yet.

It wasn't like Bangz was confirmed dead. His family had been at church the evening he went missing. But in a world infested with giant carnivorous bugs, after you were gone for eight whole days, it wasn't hard to guess what had happened to you. Just the details would remain a mystery. A mystery, or maybe a secret.

They left flowers for Bangz and Gray both. Siobhan picked them out. Milkweed. It had a special meaning that Hal couldn't remember. Then Xi started screaming out of nowhere, clawing and kicking, and Siobhan was worried she would have an asthma attack, so they had to call her mom to come pick her up.

Now, it was just the two of them. They sat side by side in Hal's Jon boat.

"How are you doing?" Hal asked.

Siobhan startled like a deer. She blinked at him. Then, she laughed. Or, at least, Hal thought it might be a laugh. It bordered on wheezing. The constriction of an airway. He remembered she had asthma, too.

"Really, really fucking bad."

It wasn't like Siobhan to curse. Hal felt the word "fucking" dig in between his ribs. It was acerbic. It pierced his heart, entered his bloodstream, and surged right into his brain stem where it kicked around his vestibular system and caused him to bowl over, rip his mask off, and vomit into the black water.

When he was done, Siobhan leaned over and hugged him. Her goggles bumped against his. He should throw up more often.

He nuzzled her back. Closed his eyes.

"You know how Bangz's family is super religious?" she whispered.

"Yeah," he whispered back.

"Once, Bangz told me and Xi that if he ever died, one of us had to pretend to get possessed by him during his funeral and scare his rich aunties into donating all their money to the Trevor Project."

Hal kept whispering. Why were they whispering? It was nice. "Did you want me to do it?"

"No. He was pretty adamant that it had to be me or Xi. I guess he thinks—thought that yours and Atlas's acting skills leave something to be desired."

"That makes sense, I guess." Hal rubbed the back of Siobhan's glove. He was careful not to use his hand with the missing finger. The one that had melted off the day Bangz died which was his fault his fault his—

"Siobhan, I..."

Siobhan didn't move. She was still leaning with her head against his shoulder. "Mhm?"

He bit his tongue and tasted blood.

No matter how much practice he got, he never got better at lying. Thom always said it was better to say nothing than stick your whole foot in your mouth. *Thom.* He hadn't seen Thom since the day Bangz died which was his fault his fault his—

They spoke at the same time:

"Did you want to come visit Atlas at the hospital?"

"Do you want to go to prom with me?"

As if she'd been bitten, Siobhan jerked upright. She'd moved so suddenly, Hal saw her almost lose balance. He reached out a hand to steady her so she wouldn't topple into the water.

She slapped his hand away. Then stood up. Again, she almost fell. Hal couldn't see her face. "Siobhan, I—"

"Don't touch me, Hal. I'm serious."

"I'm sorry. I shouldn't have asked. I'll go with you to see—"

Siobhan stepped from his boat onto hers.

"Siobhan, I'm sorry. I'm stupid. I'm fucking stupid."

"Hal, if you keep talking, I'm going to lose it. Stop talking."

"I want to see Atlas. Please. Is he okay? You said he tried to kill himself?"

Her motor stalled. She kicked it.

"I don't know why I said it. I'm fucked up. I'm sorry."

She ripped her glove off.

"Siobhan. Please. Say something."

Started messing with the motor's wires. Something sparked.

"I'm sorry. I'm sorry. I promise I'll stop talking if you—"

Finally, it roared to life.

Hal's hand flew out and grabbed the edge of her boat in a last ditch effort to stop her. A stabbing pain from his finger stub made him hiss. He instinctively recoiled, gripping it.

She didn't, in the end, say anything.

The sun went down more slowly than usual. Everything was happening slow, like the worst parts of his life were getting trapped in pitch. When he got home, Hal checked Signal and found he'd been blocked. Not just by Siobhan, but by Xi, too.

Once, there had been six of them. Now, it was just him. Alone.

"Keep crying like that, kid, and you're gonna puke."

Fingers tousled Hal's hair. Hal, suffocating with his face in a pillow, looked up. Thom was beside him in bed, playing with a dead dragonfly. Pieces of its prismatic wings were flaking off onto his sheets.

Their sheets.

"I'm going to kill myself," Hal said.

Thom, in answer, took a deep inhale. He dropped the dragonfly. "Be honest. Do you have a plan?"

"Yeah. I'm going to blow my fucking head off—"

Fingers pinched Hal's cheek. He tried to push Thom away, but Thom was stronger. Maybe it was because he had eaten Bangz. That day, by the time Hal realized—*really* realized—what was happening, Bangz was just a puddle of viscera.

His air gun lived in Hal's dresser drawer now. But a few desiccant BBs wouldn't be enough.

"Kill me, Thom. Kill me, kill me, kill me."

After a bit of wrestling, Thom had him squarely pinned. "You're cute when you're sad," he said.

Hal shuddered out a breath. Something hard was rubbing against his groin. He wanted to cry, but he was out of juice.

"Move in with me, Hal. I'll take care of you." Thom's tongue entered Hal's mouth.

It was the perfect texture. Soft, wet. Invasive. You couldn't deny it felt good. Probably, feeling good was what mattered. Thom was right. Hal was eighteen years old, still living with his mom. He'd forgotten that the Peace Corps had shuttered years ago.

Twenty-two minutes later, he let Thom have his way. It was as close to dying as he could get.

⊙

Oregon State Police

Missing Persons

Search filter - Download as csv

Page 1 / 1043

MORGAN, ISAAC L. - Photo Not Available

Age: 28 | Sex: M | Race: WHITE | Hair: BROWN | Eye Color: BROWN | Height: 5'7" | Weight: 150 | County: LANE | Date of Last Contact: 1/12/2031

HUNT, CANDICE "CANDY" - Photo Available

Age: 63 | Sex: F | Race: BLACK | Hair: GRAY OR PARTIALLY GRAY | Eye Color: BROWN | Height: 5'6" | Weight: 170 | County: LANE | Date of Last Contact: 1/13/2031

CRUZ, IRA - Photo Not Available
Age: 9 | Sex: F | Race: WHITE | Hair: BLOND OR STRAWBERRY | Eye Color: HAZEL | Height: 4'1" | Weight: 55 | County: LANE | Date of Last Contact: 01/24/2031

JAMES, ASHLYN - Photo Not Available
Age: 30 | Sex: F | Race: WHITE | Hair: RED OR AUBURN| Eye Color: GREEN | Height: 5'4" | Weight: 165 | County: LANE | Date of Last Contact: 01/26/2031

BAKER, TIMOTHY S. - Photo Not Available
Age: 47 | Sex: M | Race: UNKNOWN| Hair: UNKNOWN OR COMPLETELY BALD | Eye Color: BLUE | Height: 6'2" | Weight: 190 | County: LANE | Date of Last Contact: 02/02/2031

REYES, BARRON "BANGZ" - Photo Available
Age: 18 | Sex: M | Race: ASIAN OR PACIFIC ISLANDER | Hair: BLACK | Eye Color: BROWN | Height: 5'9" | Weight: 160 | County: LANE | Date of Last Contact: 02/07/2031

NIEFFER, HENRY "HAL" - Photo Available
Age: 18 | Sex: M | Race: WHITE | Hair: BLACK | Height: 6'0" | Eye Color: BROWN | Weight: 180 | County: LANE | Date of Last Contact: 02/13/2031

Help us improve! Was this page helpful? Yes | No

⊙

One month left, Atlas thought. *Then I'll kiss this shithole goodbye.*

He zoned out at the cattails flying by.

He anticipated not enjoying prom. What a surprise when his prediction proved true. Oliver's cyber cruiser broke down part of the way there. Their group had to slog through the mud for twenty minutes to reach the warehouse. His tux was damp with sweat by the time he peeled off his gear. Nobody could confirm for him whether any of the food at the venue was peanut-free. A realist, he was right about most things.

Except, apparently, about what color of tie to wear.

"Oof," Xi said, grimacing at it.

"Get your eyes checked." Atlas adjusted his tie—a cheerful yellow—and then shuffled to the punch bowl, which he decided he would hang around for the remainder of the evening, helped by the fact that he had a flask of vodka in his pocket.

Music assailed his eardrums. Thankfully, he'd brought earplugs. He gazed past the strobe lights. Everyone was grinding against everyone else, ass to crotch to ass. It was like witnessing a Fisher-Price orgy. A mating ball of juvenile Epicureans.

Don't be such a wet blanket, babes, a familiar voice said.

Someone squeezed his shoulder. Atlas turned. Siobhan was beside him, smiling and pointing at the dance floor where Xi had both her hands up. They said something he didn't catch. He shrugged.

"COME DANCE WITH US," Xi yelled after successfully digging out one of his earplugs.

"I think not." Atlas sipped his punch. It was more like 2 percent punch, 98 percent Smirnoff.

Siobhan gave him a knowing look. What exactly did she know? He was too buzzed to care. Twenty minutes later, he was too tipsy to care. Another twenty minutes later, he was too hammered to care. That was how it should be. Sobriety was so very tedious.

"Next thing y'know, baby got low-low-low-low-low-low-low-low—"

Popping his earplug back in, Atlas applied his mouth straight to his flask. Much better.

Seemed he wasn't the only one who loathed being sober. A kid drunkenly collided with him, then kept staggering away, head lolling. Tall. Dressed casually for prom night. Actually, dressed like a troglodyte. A ripped hoodie covered in black stains. The guy looked a lot like Hal. The spitting image of how Atlas imagined Hal's corpse looked digesting in some werm's stomach. Another friend, dead. Grief was tedious, too.

Remind me what school you got into?

Surprising himself, Atlas answered aloud, "Stanford."

Environmental science. What a waste.

"I'm not making an OnlyFans, if that's what you're implying, Bangz."

But Bangz was dead. Strange, then, that Atlas could see him standing right there, smiling that goofy smile of his that made Atlas want to throttle him. Bangz was always so smug, even when he wasn't around to be.

Atlas peered down at his drink. It was iridescent. Like soap.

Perhaps grippy socks were in order. "Is this a break with reality?" he asked.

Bangz nodded. His smile was gone.

"Hug me," Atlas said.

No time. There's something important I need to tell you—

"I said," Atlas said, snatching Bangz by his ridiculous bow-tie, "fucking hug me."

No use. Bangz never did what he was told.

Baby, you gotta listen. Bangz pointed at the glowing exit sign. *Go that way.*

"Outside? In what, this?" Atlas tugged the sleeve of his fancy-pants suit. He laughed. It was an ugly laugh. A guffaw. "I want to dance with you, you fucking simpleton."

Bangz shook his head. No, he was saying. Not this time.

Take my hand.

Atlas always did what he was told. That was his Achilles' heel.

He took Bangz's hand and let Bangz lead him. Together, they zigzagged around the sticky dance floor puddled with punch, zipped past the speakers screaming bloody murder, all the way over to the warehouse's exit. The double doors were made of reinforced steel. Acid-proof. Not even on prom night were you allowed to forget you lived during the End Times.

Okay, bud—

"Don't call me bud, fuckhead."

Okay, handsome. Almost there.

Atlas sagged against the door. His nerves sparked against the cool metal. What the hell was in that punch? Ketamine? He was seeing music, feeling it all over, especially in his hypogastric region. "I wish I never fucked you," he groaned.

No reply. Atlas didn't need to open his eyes to know Bangz was gone for good. He fought gravity and, after locking his knees, put both hands on the door's handles. He pulled.

No movement. He pushed instead. They didn't budge.

The hinges, the door frame—every square inch was coated in what looked like Elmer's glue.

Everyone knew xenopillar slime was tough as nails when it hardened. Its Achilles' heel was that it dissolved in water. If it weren't for the hallucinogenic part, xenopillars likely wouldn't have gotten much traction taking over the planet. They'd have made decent hypoallergenic pets.

"Tonight's gonna be a chill night. Tonight's gonna be a chill, chill, chill, chill, chill—"

Atlas looked down at his feet. There was red all over his shoes and hands. Red stained the floors and walls. He licked his palm.

Blood. It dawned on him then that the music he was tuning out might be the sound of people screaming.

⊙

"Are you sure I'm allowed to be here, kid?"

Hal rolled his eyes. "Stop calling me 'kid.' I have fifteen years over you."

The music in the venue was loud. So loud, Hal could feel it from all the way out here. He checked his reflection in the still water at his feet. Turned his head left, right, up, down. A month of refraining from picking his sores and his skin was finally healing.

Fidget toys were a good substitute for therapy. Especially when running away from home meant you lost your health insurance.

"Just answer the question, Hal."

Frogs were hiccuping all around them. The sun was almost down. Hal could feel his skin prickling from mosquitoes. He squeezed a cattail in his hand. "I want you here."

"Alright. If you say so." Thom stepped out from behind a tree. "How, uh. How do I look?"

Thirty seconds passed. Hal coughed. "Good," he said finally.

Thom's smile fell. He started fumbling with his tie. "You're not gonna gas me up even a little? You should know I'm going out of my comfort zone here."

You're cute when you're nervous, Hal nearly said. Ugh. The pre-gaming they'd done was getting to him.

He walked over, careful not to get mud onto his suit. It wasn't easy keeping clean when you were bumming it out at a 7-Eleven. He fixed Thom's tie. He also fixed his hair, which had a few leaves poking out at the top. "You wear nice clothes all the time. More than anyone else I know."

"Yeah, but I don't meet new people that often. I'm shy."

Hal flicked him between the eyes. "You're not shy. You're introverted. Don't get them confused."

"Hey, don't flick me. I'm your date. You gotta treat me right."

They walked up to the venue's doors. It was an old warehouse that had been repurposed for events like these. Prom night. Graduation was just around the corner. Hal put a hand on the door.

His heart pounded.

"You sure you'll be okay?" Thom nosed his cheek. His breath smelled wet. "You and your friends had that falling out. What if they recognize you?"

"That's the point, Thom. I want them to see me." Hal took a deep breath. No one had ever warned him about how fast you grew up once you left the nest. Once you were an adult, there was no going back. "After this, I'll go home and see Mom. I'll apologize. For everything."

Thom's eyes bugged. "Everything?"

"Yeah. Everything."

"Okay. But don't apologize for Bangz dying. That was all me."

"It was my decision not to tell anyone about it. Can you blame them for cutting me off? I'm a creep. I'd cut me off, too." Hal sighed. He raked a hand through his hair. "I just hope they won't hate me forever."

He was yanking the door open when Thom's hand flew out and stopped him.

"Don't forget, I'm still two years older than you in human years." Those red eyes twinkled. Thom's smile was blinding. "Can I give you some advice?"

Talking like an old man when he was barely twenty. Thom couldn't even legally drink yet. Or rent a vehicle. *This better be good.* "Shoot," Hal said.

Thom winked. "Just because something's not real"—he tapped Hal's chest with a finger—"doesn't mean it doesn't matter."

Sure. Like time and Bitcoin.

Gentleman that he was, Thom held the door open and beckoned Hal inside.

To Hal's surprise, they actually had a good time, though. It turned out nobody hated him. And everyone loved Thom, much to Thom's obvious delight. Attention whore. The guy was such a serial fucking liar. When they got to Hal's house, Hal's mom cried a little, and then

Thom told her that he and Hal met at the DMV. Who meets anyone at the DMV?

"May I have this dance?" Thom asked, extending a hand.

Hal blinked. "I thought we went home."

"We are home," Thom said. He snapped his fingers, and it began to rain. "C'mon, Hal. It's the last song."

You had to admit, Thom was handsome. He looked good in white. He looked good even when he was soaked to the bone in an oversize tux, with that one leaf poking out of his hair that Hal had apparently missed. Hal only wished he'd stop winking all the time. It made him seem devious. But he'd apologized a million times for eating Bangz. No, Thom wasn't a bad guy. It was just that he didn't have a supportive family or friends. Not like Hal had always had. Growing up, you made mistakes. You learned from them. Thom would learn, just like Hal would learn. The brain was plastic. You had to build new pathways. Don't give up. Not even when things look *really, really fucking bad.* Which, right now, for the first time in what felt like forever, they somehow didn't.

Smiling, Hal took Thom's hand. From behind, he heard a *ch-chck.*

He turned. Guns were dangerous. You really didn't want to be swinging one around loaded. Especially not pointed at someone's prom date.

Thankfully, it wasn't a shotgun Siobhan was holding. Just Bangz's dinky air pistol.

Still. Could take an eye out.

Siobhan was wearing the most beautiful dress Hal had ever seen. A million colors, but mostly blue. Probably, it would look better if it weren't so waterlogged. She needed a coat over her shoulders, but Hal wasn't going to touch her. He had learned his lesson.

Thom was being awfully quiet. Understandable.

"Hi, Siobhan." Hal tried to smile. He thought he had already introduced them, but that was fine, he didn't mind doing it again. "This is Thom. Thom, meet—"

Siobhan raised the shotgun that wasn't a shotgun, thank god.

Great. There was awkwardness simmering between them. Maybe an apology would help? "I'm sorry," Hal said. It probably didn't sound sincere. That's because he was learning how not to apologize for things he wasn't sorry for.

"Get back, Hal," Siobhan said.

Thom hummed. "Gonna need you to step aside for a quick sec, kid, while I take care of something."

"No. I can fix this," Hal said.

He knew exactly what to do. Thom was fast, but Hal was faster.

He threw himself between them, his best friend and his ex-best friend, who were already fighting—over something stupid, probably—and yelled "seriously, guys?" and then Thom said "oh fuck" and something went *BLAM* and when he (Hal) died, it wasn't even scary, because to be totally, perfectly honest, it wasn't the first time, and maybe, if he got lucky (which was getting to be less and less a rarity), it wouldn't be the last.

⊙

AtlasSniffed [03:29]: thank you Siobhan

AtlasSniffed [03:43]: i wouldnt be here if you hadnt come back for me

cluecat [03:45]: It was Xi who got to the sprinklers.

cluecat [03:48]: She handed me the gun.

cluecat [03:51]: I don't even know where she got it. There was so much chaos. I could barely see.

cluecat [03:52]: It doesn't feel real.

cluecat [03:58]: I miss her so much.

AtlasSniffed [04:39]: i saw Bangz

cluecat [04:45]: I saw him too. He snapped me out of it.

AtlasSniffed [05:55]: i also saw Hal

AtlasSniffed [05:58]: maybe it was him. i dont know.

AtlasSniffed [05:58]: he didnt look right

AtlasSniffed [06:04]: did you see him too?

cluecat [13:02]: No. I didn't.

⊙

Hal wasn't always eighteen years old. Once, he was even eight.

If you'd have told him in five years, the world would be ending, he wouldn't have believed you. But he'd still have gotten scared. Don't tell anyone, but he slept with a night light in his room.

Embarrassing. Anyway.

It was a bad day. He had just gotten out of swim practice. Everyone was mad at him because his feet had touched the bottom of the pool while doing laps, and Coach made everyone do an extra lap. All because of him.

When he was in first grade, Coach had awarded him M.V.P. He got a trophy for it and everything.

What had changed? He was older now. The older he got, the more it seemed like people didn't like him. It was definitely the case today, with everyone giving him the stinky eye. *Thanks a lot, Nieffer.*

It was summer. His mom was late picking him up. Swaddled in a towel, teeth chattering, Hal watched the older kids magically unlock the gate at the back and climb the stairs.

He tried to follow them. That got him yelled at. So he went to the playground and punched the tetherball until, big surprise, it swung around and socked him right in the face.

He'd always been a crybaby. It was something he would eventually grow out of. But, again, he's eight here. Sitting on the concrete, bawling his eyes out. His forehead hurts. Maybe there's a hole in it.

"Yeesh. You okay, kid?"

Hal opens one eye. Standing over him is a kid older than him, staring down with a funny expression. White hair, red eyes. Or maybe he's just imagining the red part. It could be a trick of the light.

"I'm fine," Hal lies.

The older kid leaves. Then comes back with a pair of Otter Pops. One red, one blue. He holds one of the Otter Pops to Hal's head. The cold helps it not hurt as much. If there is a hole, it's probably smaller now.

"What's your name, kid?"

It's weird being called "kid" by another kid. But Hal isn't going to complain. Otter Pops are twenty-five cents each, which is twenty-five more cents than he has. He tells him his name.

"Cool. My name's Thom."

Thom pets the top of Hal's head. Gently, the way you're supposed to pet a cat. Hal doesn't think Thom is on the swim team. He's never seen Thom before. Maybe he's from Switzerland.

"You're crying again? Yeesh. You sure cry a lot."

"I want *(sniff)* to go home."

Thom takes a deep, long sigh. A dragonfly lands on the tip of his shoe. He tries to catch it with his hands, but it darts away. Then, realizing Hal is staring at him, Thom winks.

"Alright, alright. Let's get you home, kid."

"H-how?"

Thom crunches the Otter Pop with his teeth. His lips are stained red from the cherry flavor. "Uh. Okay, I got it. Close your eyes. Then, on the count of three, open 'em."

Hal closes his eyes and feels Thom overlap them with an ice-cold hand, just to make sure he won't peek. His head really doesn't hurt any more. Amazing. Thom is a magician. He waits.

"One, two, three. Now open."

Thom's hand lifts, and Hal opens his eyes. He guessed Thom was pulling his leg, but what do you know, he hadn't lied. Even though

Hal is just a gullible kid who can be convinced to believe just about anything.

End.

ABOUT THE AUTHOR

Piamo (they/them) is a small birb with a stuffy nose.

https://piamo.neocities.org
https://bsky.app/profile/piamo.bsky.social
https://piamo.beehiiv.com
https://patreon.com/ppiamo

ALSO BY PIAMO

I can be your angle or your devil (b ˙W˙)b

RETURN TO THE WORLD!

RETURN TO THE WORLD!

Count down to Christmas with a silly BL novella!

RETURN TO
RETURN TO THE WORLD!

The gang's back! And now the MC is... Gabriel?!!

STANDALONE

HURT TO KILL

An alien ambassador.
An unlikely friend.
A grieving king.

【*There is no greater monster than memory.*】

NEGATIVE RESIST

It's not as clean in here as it should be.

Two engineers fuck nasty in a semiconductor cleanroom. MM pairing + omegaverse setting. 9k word short story. Free to read on itchio.

TRIVIAL MEET-CUTE

During a night of bar trivia, a brush with death brings three men together.

A morbid but lighthearted 8.8k word short story. If you subscribe to my newsletter, you get this one free.

Made in the USA
Coppell, TX
19 June 2026

81858423R00049